Midnight with Mimi

By

Joanne Dillard Addison

Illustrated by

Jessica Lawrence

This book belongs to:

_____

To order additional copies of this book, contact:
Xlibris Corporation
1-888-795-4274
www.Xlibris.com
Orders@Xlibris.com

Dedication

This book is dedicated to my
ten favorite grandchildren.
I love their parents and I love them.
I wouldn't be Mimi without them.

I also love their names:

Julianna, who gave me my nickname

Elizabeth, who gave me continuous encouragement and named the book

Marianna, who is my email buddy and pal

Jonathan, who is my Lovett School #67 football player

Matthew, who is my TALL loving grandson

Daniel, who is my computer expert

Caroline, who was my "Bug-hunting" partner

Spencer, who is my UGA pal, helper, and friend

Allison Dillard, who is my namesake

Stewart, who is my youngest grandbaby, big and handsome

I wish to thank the following people, for without their help,

then this little book would not have been written.

Sharon Jollay, who got things started,

Pat Sartain, with her talents and skills,

Leisa Jones, who saw talent in the illustrator,

and helped the two of us to form a book partnership team,

Amy Lyford, the author's photographer,

Roy Jones and the Galaxy Diner,

for letting us use the restaurant for our meetings,

Jim Nall, the book's computer expert,

and friend, Ken White, and Chick-Fil-A

for being the first book-signing location,

Ron and Joyce Swafford with their publishing skills

in Conasauga Publishing and Educational Consulting LLC,

and my life long good friend, Carl Griffin, who kept things moving along.

THANK YOU   THANK YOU   THANK YOU

MIDNIGHT WITH MIMI

WRITTEN BY JOANNE DILLARD ADDISON

ILLUSTRATED BY JESSICA LAWRENCE

CHAPTERS

Chapter I
Mimi To the Rescue ♥

nce upon a time–yes, when I was a little girl, learning to read, nearly all books that I read (or that mama and daddy read to me) started out with "Once upon a time"– and most books ended with "and they all lived happily ever after." Sooooo, since this book is a book . . . it shall begin as follows:

Once upon a time, in a sweet little bedroom, in a sweet little home, in a sweet little town called "Tuckertown," in the sweet little state of Georgia, all was quiet until . . .

I was awakened suddenly from a deep and peaceful sleep by the sound of someone crying softly down the hall. I crawled out of my snug bed to see what was the matter.

Now, I am a mother of five and a grandmother of ten. On this particular night, my baby daughter and one of my four "favorite" sons-in-law (her hubby) and their three beautiful children from Texas were visiting with us in Tuckertown.

You should have seen me "tiptoeing" down the hall in the dark, with no shoes on, wearing a short blue night gown and toting my trusty red-and-black Georgia flashlight. I would have scared the "Boogie Man" himself if he had seen me. Why, I even scared myself! I peered down the dark hall, shining my flashlight from side to side. Someone was coming towards me with a flashlight! Phew! It was just my reflection in the floor-door mirror. I was still afraid, though, because I was not used to hearing someone cry out in the dark, in the middle of the night.

The clock struck 12–'twas midnight. It was raining and it was dark. I mean really, really dark. Sooo dark that I couldn't tell one shadow from another. I peeped into the bedroom on my right and was able to locate the bed. Soon, my trusty red-and-black Georgia flashlight shone upon the lovely face of my ten-year old granddaughter, Caroline. She had tears streaming from her eyes. She was sobbing uncontrollably as though her heart was broken.

"Caroline," I asked, "why are you crying in the middle of the night?"

Her answer was simple. She said that she had tippy-toed to her mama's bedroom to let her know that she had been awakened by the hard rain and she could not go back to sleep. She told me that her mom ignored her at first, and then fussed at her, telling her to go back to bed, because it was "the middle of the night."

Apparently, this made Caroline sob louder, and that's when I had heard the cry in the dark. It sounded to me like a cry for help. Any kind of help from anyone available... soooo...

MIMI TO THE RESCUE!

"Caroline," I assured her, "your mama wasn't fussing at you. She was just letting you know that it's midnight, and time for all good little boys and girls to be in bed, sound asleep."

Despite my consoling words, Caroline continued to sob because she felt as though the whole world had turned against her.

With a puzzled expression on her face, she looked up at me through her tears and asked, "Mimi, why are you awake in the middle of the night, with no shoes on, wearing a thin, short blue night gown and shining your trusty red-and-black Georgia flashlight up and down the hall?"

I calmly thought and then spoke. "Caroline," I said, "I am looking for BUGS! They come out after dark, you know."

I truly don't know why I said "BUGS" because I really hate BUGS. Why, even talking about BUGS makes me shiver with fear.

Desperate to see a smile on her face, I asked, "Would you like to come join me?"

Caroline never even flinched. "Sure!" she said as she leaped out of her bed and wiped away the tears. Mimi apparently had come to the rescue, and now the only thing to do was to hunt for BUGS.

Needless to say, Caroline had to be given a trusty red-and-black Georgia flashlight to use on a "first-of-a-kind Bug-hunting adventure," way past midnight with Mimi in the dark Tuckertown.

Chapter II
Dancing On Raindrops

ave you ever been up in the middle of the night, when it was sooo dark that you couldn't see one hand in front of the other? Well, we were!

We knew that we couldn't make any noise because we didn't want to wake anyone up. We also knew that we were supposed to be in bed and, by now, sound asleep. So, we tippy-toed into the big den (across from the little den) and closed the door slightly. We looked at each other and quietly giggled. We took turns shining the trusty red-and-black Georgia flashlight underneath our chins. This was so funny to us because it made our beautiful faces UGLY! Yes, I mean U_G_L_Y!!!!

We never turned on a light for fear of waking someone. We continued to shine our flashlights on the walls and ceilings. Heaven forbid if a BUG had come out (since it was after DARK), and had fallen on our heads and landed in our hair, on its way down from the ceiling to the ground. We surely would have screamed!

We took turns shining our trusty red-and-black Georgia flashlights up and down and all around.

Next, we decided to go out on the wet-floored deck. The air was warm, fresh-smelling, and moist to the skin. The sky was black. The wind was gently blowing. Things were calm in Tuckertown after the rain.

We began to hop from one rain puddle to another. This was soooo much fun! We knew that we weren't supposed to be outside the house—but, we also knew that our backyard was fenced in and we were safe. No one else was up because it was past midnight and everyone was sound asleep—yes, it was past midnight—way past midnight—way, way, past midnight!

15

We danced on the deck—yes, we danced on the rain drops, with no light except the light from the stars in the night sky. We danced in circles, freely waving our arms and hopping like frogs. We strutted like majorettes leading a band in a parade. We waved our trusty red-and-black Georgia flashlights in circles and made odd designs in the air. We wrote the alphabet in space. We giggled softly because we didn't wish to wake anyone. We knew that if we did, we would surely get fussed at!

Chapter III
Ottoman Time

ave you ever been up in the middle of the night—way, way past midnight when it was so dark that you bumped into furniture? Well, we did! We even bumped into each other! Yes, and when we bumped into each other, Caroline fell down next to the bookshelf. We laughed silently, because it was way, way past midnight, and we did not want to wake anyone.

The light from Caroline's trusty red-and-black Georgia flashlight shown upon her parents' and aunts' wedding albums. She had looked at them many times before, but it just seemed the thing to do now, in the dark, on the floor of the very big den (across from the little den).

Being a mother of five and a grandmother of ten, I could not get down on the floor "Indian style" as Caroline could. I have always said that she has legs like her dad. I call their legs "good-looking rubber legs" because they fold up and go wherever you want them to, just like a rubber band.

Of course, I love for the grandchildren to see the wedding albums, and I jump at every chance for them to "have the opportunity" to view them.

Meanwhile, I went back into the little den and got my favorite $250.00 ottoman. This little ottoman has been worth every red penny that it cost, because all grandchildren and step-grandchildren have played on it, rolled on it, kicked it, and just down-right enjoyed it!

The ottoman was just the thing! I sat on it, while Caroline thumbed through wedding albums, making whispering comments about how her aunts and uncles looked so young back then, and how now, they looked so old. I thought to myself that Caroline must see me, too, through her eyes as being "Old as Methuselah!" (a phrase my mother, affectionately known as "Momee," used often.)

Shhhh! I thought I heard a noise! I listened carefully . . . Oh well, it was gone . . .

What a wonderful time we were having. Don't you wonder how Caroline landed on the floor right next to the bookshelf with the wedding albums? I suppose she could have been guided towards that particular bookshelf . . . . I wonder who would have done such a thing? We will never know, because it was soooo dark, and I'll never tell . . . .

We finally grew tired of flipping through the wedding albums. The time had come to put them away and continue our bug search. We headed towards the deck door which had been left open for Crystal to come and go as she pleased. Crystal is our twelve-pound Pekingese dog, the queen of our home and the baby of Brownlee Drive in Tuckertown.

All of a sudden, a dark shadow appeared from nowhere. There was stillness everywhere. You could have heard a pin drop. We both shined our lights towards the den! What was that tinkling noise?

Aha! It was only Crystal! The identification coins on her collar gave her location away. The "queen" had been outside, and we thought that she had been in her bed, sound asleep, as all good little dogs were supposed to be. We let her in and locked the door. If any BUGS had come in the house, we would surely get them!

Oddly enough, I was still hearing strange and unnecessary noises, pops, low sounding squeaks, almost as though someone or something was creeping around on the carpet.

Fortunately for us, we saw NO BUGS! However, BUGS do come out after dark, you know!

Chapter IV
The Biography Of
Joanne Dillard Addison

aroline and I yawned and sighed, but, we were not ready for bed. No, not just yet. It was fun being up past midnight—way, way past midnight, in the dark, supposedly hunting for bugs. We giggled some more and played "I'm going to California and I'm taking a..." with the alphabet and our keen memorization skills. After that we softly sang our favorite childhood songs until we could sing no more.

I knew we were getting tired, because we weren't giggling nearly so much now. Caroline found a paper titled "The Biography of Joanne Dillard Addison." She yawned several more times before she said, "This little booklet looks interesting, and it's only one o'clock, so I think that I will read it aloud, but very quietly, of course, because I do not want to wake up anyone in the house."

I was so proud listening to her read to me. When she was younger, I had read to her. I couldn't believe how much she had grown up since her last visit.

I wonder who had placed this particular piece of interesting work on the bottom bookshelf? I'll never tell...

There goes that mysterious sound again. Hmmmm....

Here are the exact words that were printed in large bold black print, written three years ago.

THE BIOGRAPHY OF
JOANNE DILLARD ADDISON

Have you ever heard about Joanne Addison? Well, she is my grandmother and she is really funny. I can't go to her house without cracking up. This biography will tell you all about her life.

Hey! Did you know she was born on Feb. 16, 1938 in Rome, GA? I think that was a long time ago. Well, she is 66 years old so I guess it is. Can you believe she has five children! The first girl is Melinda. The second girl is Monica. The next girl is Anna Marie, but we call her Marie. Finally, they had a boy. His name is Roger. Then there is my mother, Michelle. My grandmother has one dog. Her name is Crystal! She is a really pretty dog. Now you know about her at home, why not go to school?

First of all, Joanne went to South Rome School for her elementary years. She loved 3rd grade! After lunch her teacher would let her go outside and draw under an oak tree where she could see her. In high school, her worst subject was Math! She just couldn't do the problems. Joanne had a best friend named Carolyn and they did everything together. They even had the same hobbies! Do you want to hear them?

Joanne loved to dance. She took dance lessons all her life. Tap, Jazz, you name it! She also loved to take pictures. She would look back at pictures she had taken and said it was history! She would collect things a lot too. Joanne is a pack rat. That means she doesn't want to throw anything away. Joanne also had lots of adventures too.

Joanne was a majorette in high school. That is the person in the front of a parade waving a baton! She even led the parade where it's supposed to go. Another fact is that she was camper of the week! Out of 500 kids, she was picked! I think this is pretty cool. My grandmother said, "I was happy when I was blessed with 5 children and 9 grandchildren."

(Remember, Mimi has ten grandchildren, and this was written before Stewart was born.)

Joanne is also afraid of things like bugs.

(There was a reason to have you read this part of the biography. See, it ties in together with that old word BUGS. Pretty smart, huh?)

Joanne has a fear of spiders. Probably because some are poisonous. Speaking of bugs, she really hates roaches! Here is an animal she hates. Snakes! And I agree, they are nasty.

Another thing that you want to know about is traveling. If she could go anywhere in the world it would be Rome, Georgia. She said so herself. It is her hometown!

Joanne wants to be healthy so she can attend her grandchildren's college graduations and weddings. I would like to say a few words.

I dedicated this book to you, Mimi, and I want you to know I wrote it with love!

Written by Caroline

Caroline was so surprised that she had written this little booklet! She said that she had not remembered writing it. But she liked it, and I loved it! Time moved on— the darkness was still there. Yawns became more frequent. Rubbing of eyes took place, but a fancy red book with gold glitter on it caught Caroline's eye—"New York 2003."

"Oh Mimi, I have never seen this book!" Caroline exclaimed.

I told her that it was a very interesting book and was put together for me by my favorite first born grandchild, Julianna, who was responsible for giving me my nickname Mimi.

Julianna had been a part of my being "kidnapped" back in 2003 for a surprise trip to New York City. This was one of the most wonderful surprises ever put over on me. It was made by my four daughters

and three oldest granddaughters. Julianna had made this scrapbook for me as a souvenir of our trip to the city. She saved pictures, coupons, passes, etc. to create this lovely remembrance book.

I wonder how the red book with the gold glitter caught her eye? All I know is that somehow my trusty red-and-black Georgia flashlight's light circled and landed right on the gold lettering. Hmmm . . .

One half hour later, we both began to yawn. The slowly dripping rain drops had ceased long ago. It was my time to make a suggestion.

"Caroline, I know what we could do! Since it is way, way, way, past midnight," I said, "we could always play checkers even though we've never really played checkers in the dark before."

Soooo, we played. She won! I was black and she was red. We played again. She won! I was red, she was black. She won. We played again. She won again.

I made another suggestion. "Caroline, how about us going nighty-night?"

BUT this was not what she had in her sleepy little mind. We both were really tired, but I think that deep down we both wanted to just stay awake as long as we could.

Anyway, to make a long story short . . . a final suggestion was made by Caroline. I went along with this suggestion, except that I suggested chocolate syrup to be poured on my dish of vanilla ice cream! Now you know what the suggestion was, don't you?

Yes, we sat in the dark den, with our trusty red-and-black Georgia flashlights propped on the table. We needed both hands, because we didn't just mess around and get a small dip of ice cream. No siree! We did it up just right. I served Caroline one of Mimi's BIG-sized scoops! In comparison, my bowl looked like a bowl of chocolate syrup with only a small scoop of vanilla ice cream. It took both hands for us to eat our 2:30 a.m. snack.

Have you ever eaten ice cream in the dark in the middle of the night? Try it. You may like it!

Chapter V

The Ice Cream Did It !

ea! Bedtime had finally arrived. We did not want to wake anyone in the house, so Caroline and I tippy-toed to her bedroom in the dark without our trusty red-and-black Georgia flashlights on.

I started to tuck Caroline back into bed. Oops, not so fast! Caroline wanted to go brush her teeth. We both shook our heads NO, and I continued to pull covers up over her and

fluff her pillow. We gently pushed her little sister, Allison, over because she had rolled to the middle of the bed they were sharing.

Caroline turned on her flashlight for the last time that evening. This time she was shining it on the floor beside the bed.

"Mimi, Look!" She declared, "NO BUGS!"

"Mimi, I'm sleepy," she said as she yawned. "I guess the ice cream did it!"

A hug and a kiss and "God, bless everyone" was quietly spoken. Soon, there were four eyes closed and two sweet little gals sound asleep. It was 2:45ish. The rain had completely stopped, the sky was dark, and Crystal, the dog, was curled up in her little doggy bed.

Once again, I quietly walked down the hall and opened our bedroom door. My husband Larry was snoozing soundly. Even baby Stewart and his parents were sleeping undisturbed, or so it seemed. Talk about feeling blessed! I did feel blessed, and I was very, very happy with the evening's events. I was especially pleased that we had found NO BUGS!

I still heard a sound or two. Hmmm... Not the sound bugs make, I thought.

Good night, BUGS, wherever you are!

Good night, boys and girls.

Good night, Jon Boy.

Good night.

Good night.

Good night.

Chapter VI

Oops! Now What Do We Do?

ell . . . after only three hours of sleep, I turned over in the bed and looked at the clock. I could not believe that it was time to crawl out of the bed and begin my exciting morning business. I let Miss Crystal out, took my morning pill, "did my thing," saw to it that good ole' Larry got his medicine, fixed coffee for him, made the bed, bathed, put on my make-up, brushed my teeth, ate a bite of toast and got dressed. Did I mention that all these events took place while I watched my favorite TV program out of the corner of my eye? This may not sound very exciting, but have you ever done all of the above, when everyone else was asleep and I had to tippy-toe in order to remain quiet and try to not wake anyone?

I knew that everyone else in the house could sleep late. I also knew that the baby Stewart would wish to "arise and shine" way before his parents would want to get up. I had a very important early appointment, at the beauty shop, so Remza, from Bosnia, could "make me beautiful" as she did every Saturday morning.

While away from the family, my mind kept telling me that Michelle (Caroline's mom) would frown upon our frolicking in the dark, outside, on the deck, in the rain eating ice-cream, staying up past midnight, way, way, way past midnight, and not even trying to go to sleep until nearly morning. She was quite a stickler when it came to her children getting a good night's sleep. They knew the routine, she said, and they were supposed to follow it.

I thought to myself, "Now, we are in deep trouble."

"What do we do, oh, what do we do? What would you do?"

Well, I called Caroline from the beauty shop and her mother answered the phone. This made matters even worse. My tummy was nervous. I wanted to do the right thing. After all, I was an adult. I was the one who was supposed to set a good example, not stir up trouble.

Was it too late? I set an example all right last night, didn't I. Sure I did! After Caroline's mom told her to go to bed and go to sleep, I let her stay up and "hunt for bugs in the dark," way past midnight, way, way, way past midnight.

In the past, when the grandchildren wanted to stay up, I would always try to talk to and reason with them.

"It is bedtime and time for all good little boys and girls to be in the bed."

The reasoning always seemed to work. But, last night, I had said something different, and even though I dearly HATE BUGS, at that moment, it seemed to be the right thing to say. Oh why, oh why did we stay up way, way, way past midnight? All grandmothers should have been in bed early, because grandparents get tired, faster than young "whipper snappers" do.

Anyway, Caroline's mom was surprised that I wanted to speak to Caroline so early on the phone and that I would not tell her what I wanted to say.

Caroline was put on the phone. I told her exactly how I felt, and as it turned out, she had been thinking the same thing, too. That is why she had not mentioned the whole "bug thing" to her mom. I tell you, we both felt guilty, as we should have (maybe).

Sooo, for the time being, we said that we had a secret, and no one, we meant *no one*, would know it, until we decided that we would tell the secret to all. First things first. Mimi to the Rescue, I said to myself. Better talk with Caroline's mother and, then, find out her feelings concerning the "Midnight with Mimi" episode. I had to make her promise that she will not be mad with us. Promise us that she will not scold us. In fact, if she did approve, then she should share her approval with us and then we would all be happy. I was getting a little shaky. My mouth became dry. I told myself that I must do the right thing.

I talked two more times with Caroline over the phone. When I came home, I had a big job to do. Talk to her mother, and win her over. Let her know that I am the adult, the grandmother of ten, and I have my own set of rules to follow. The bonding that took place last night between the grandmom and grandchild was well worth the TALK.

O.K, Michelle, here I come. We must speak in private—now!

Chapter VII
"Be Happy Time" is Near

hen I returned home from "getting beautiful" at Remza's beauty shop, everyone was up and either eating, playing, watching TV cartoons, making beds, feeding the baby, playing with the dog, or being loud by all talking at the same time. (Oh, this is a gift that was given to me, and I do believe that I handed this gift down to my five children and ten grandchildren). We can listen and talk—all of us at the same time, and not miss any fact in the conversations. Also, I'm proud of the gift that went along with the gift of listening and talking. This gift is laughing at the end of the sentence. We do have a tendency to laugh often after speaking. Try it. It's fun to do. This will help one stay young and have fewer wrinkles—smile, laugh, be calm, reduce stress. Who am I fooling? I do hope that Michelle will be her cute self and talk and laugh—a sincere laugh, that is.

Anyway, I had not thought of what we had done to be BAD. I did go hunting for bugs in the middle of the night, in a short, blue nightgown, with no shoes on, shining my trusty red-and-black Georgia flashlight up and down the halls, on the ceiling and the walls. This was not a lie. However, this was not the exact truth either. It just seemed to be the thing to do at that very moment. And, it worked! The family had not been bothered by it. They continued with their wonderful sleep and their pleasant dreams.

Mimi to the Rescue! I had wanted Caroline to stop crying in the middle of the night. If we had awakened Allison, then there would have been a chance that we would have been up way later than 2:45ish in the morning and then the three of us would have awakened the baby, and he would have awakened his parents, and they would have awakened good ole' Larry, and Crystal the dog would have barked and wanted to go outside. The more I think about this—all of my family should thank me for being so creative and using my "God-given original imagination" because their sleep

31

was not disturbed! Hey! Why am I feeling so concerned? Maybe I'm making a mountain out of a molehill. Oh well, I was about to find out that there really are two sides to every story. I was going to have to do some quick "reasoning" and quick thinking and talking. After all, Michelle was *my* baby and I had to "reason" with her. I had to win her over . . .

Wait and see what happened next!

Chapter VIIII

Making A Big-to-do About Nothing

y happy family continued with their usual entertainments. Michelle gave the baby to the dad, and she and I went into the bedroom and closed the door.

"What is so important that we have to be behind closed doors?" she asked.

She proceeded to tell me that Caroline had been acting strangely while I was off "getting beautiful."

I told Michelle that she needed to listen, not talk, nor laugh, until I was through with my "practiced speech." Then, Caroline could come in and give her "practiced speech."

I thought to myself, "I'm really making such a BIG TO-DO about nothing—No, perhaps, I'm not!"

I again said to myself, "We may have not followed the rules, but, we bonded more, and had so much fun, and we did not bother anyone—oh well—we'll see . . . Here goes . . . ."

"Honey," I said, "first of all, what I am fixing to tell you is not BAD. Caroline and I feel

as though we did wrong because she did not obey your request to return to her bed and go back to sleep last night. I found her sobbing and thought that since I was up, I might be able to help her to be happy again. I tried to "reason" with her but to no avail. That is when the whole "Bug-hunting" idea came to me—from out of nowhere. I simply tried it and it worked."

"Honey," I continued, "you know that I would not let anything bad happen to Caroline. She and I knew that we were supposed to be in our beds for the night. But, we were so happy and having sooo much fun. We didn't know that we would be up for three hours past midnight. We were wide awake!"

"Caroline and I did not feel as though we were not following your directions. Time just flew by, and when we did get sleepy, we realized that we had not kept up with the clock. We had so much going on. We felt safe and happy, and again, may I repeat, we were wide awake, very safe, and very happy with our "BUG hunt"!

"You ask me what "BUG hunt"! Well, I'll tell you. When Caroline continued to sob after leaving your bedroom at midnight, I, Mimi, came to the Rescue. I calmed her down when I told her why I was up, in the dark, with no shoes on, in a short blue nightgown and shining my trusty red-and-black Georgia flashlight up and down the hall. I asked her if she wanted to join me in my search for hunting BUGS, and when she said very quickly, "Sure!" then our evening of fun began! One thing led to another. We did so many fun things. We not only "hunted for bugs," we danced on the rain drops on the deck in the middle of the night with no shoes on, played checkers in the dark, and by the light of my trusty red-and-black Georgia flashlight, sang the "A, you're adorable" song, looked at wedding albums and ate great big Mimi-sized ice cream sundaes!"

I told Michelle that there are always two sides to every story and asked her if she would like to tell me how she actually felt right now. I questioned the fact that she had a right to be mad, or maybe the word I should have used was *disappointed*, with us, just because we did not honor her demand to send Caroline back to bed. After all, it was midnight in dark Tuckertown and almost everyone was in bed asleep. But, on the other hand, Caroline was in the care of her grandmother, and grandmoms have a tendency of "giving in" and spoiling the grandchildren. But this is O.K. After all, Grandmoms can and have earned the right to spoil their grandchildren.

"Please, Michelle," I pleaded, "Do you see our side of the story?"

Chapter IX

You Seemed To Be Having Sooo Much Fun!

he suspense was killing me. Would Michelle really see our side of the story?

"Wow," Michelle finally answered! "Mom, you have put me between the devil and the deep blue sea." (This is an expression that means a person is being caught in the middle of a problem.) She coughed, cleared her throat, coughed again, took a deep breath, sighed, giggled, frowned, smiled, kept silent, looked away, intentionally made no eye-to-eye contact with me and then wiped her face with a tissue. It seemed as though she "had the floor" so to speak, but she remained silent, staring into space. This seemed to have lasted a long time, but really it wasn't very long at all.

She never did say that we were guilty. When she finally spoke, I couldn't believe my ears!

"Repeat that please," I said. "I don't think I heard you correctly."

What do you think her answer was? Did she choose sides? Was she mad at us? Was she unhappy with us for not obeying bedtime orders? Was she cool and calm in her "unprepared speech"? Remember now that Caroline and I both had "prepared" our speeches, while Michelle was "on her own," so to speak, searching for words out of the blue. You will soon learn her answer. And I can tell you that I was very surprised, yet happy! This may give you a hint.

I told Michelle that I would go get Caroline to join us in our friendly, three-generational meeting, or shall I say get-together. My smile made Caroline happy as she entered the room. In other parts of the house, everyone else was still doing his or her own thing—feeding the baby, watching TV cartoons, eating, talking, giggling, laughing, reading, etc.

"Caroline," I said, "you and I have worried and worried for no reason. Your mom is truly a good sport. She said that—oh, I can't tell you what she said, so I want you to guess what she said about our BUG situation. Guess out loud, Caroline, guess out loud!"

But before Caroline had a chance to say anything, Michelle told her, "I am jealous, Caroline, at what fun you two had last night for three long hours. All I can say is that Mimi never let me stay up late to hunt for bugs in the dark, or dance on the rain drops, or play checkers by the light of a trusty red-and-black Georgia flashlight, or sing silly songs, or eat ice cream with lots and lots of chocolate syrup on it in the dark in the middle of the night. Way, way, way, past midnight, I might add I am jealous! You two seemed to be having soooo much fun!"

What Michelle didn't know is that if the same situation had ever arisen when she was a little girl, I would most definitely have gone along with it.

Chapter X
Can You Believe This?
A Live Spy!

an you believe this? Caroline's mom was actually jealous because we were up way past midnight and having so much fun. However, it did seem as though Michelle didn't know what to say about our apologies and our feelings of guilt.

Why? I wondered. I noticed that she, too, appeared a tad guilty herself. I didn't know why. She rolled her eyes again, she looked away, she coughed, and she sighed, but all the while she remained silent.

Why did she appear so confused? She had given us an answer that made us happy. Why did we feel that something was wrong? We had confessed. We felt better. But, still, something was not right.

Something was definitely bothering Michelle. She didn't talk fast and laugh at the end of the sentence like she always had done in the past.

I started "putting two and two together" and whispered to Caroline that I thought her mom was acting a bit odd. We both noticed the quick personality change. Now, I'm not a detective, but I am a grandmother of ten with a creative imagination and plenty of ideas of my own.

I leaned over again and whispered to Caroline that her mother must have a secret concerning our BUG project. "Now that I think about it," I said softly, "she sure had a strange look on her face when we told her that we felt as though she should have been with us last night for the first-of-a-kind "Bug-hunting" adventure."

Again, Michelle said, "Ya'll looked like you were having soooo much fun!"

What did she mean, "We looked like we were having so much fun?"

"Michelle," I asked point-blank, "were you awake last night, hiding in the dark without a trusty red-and-black Georgia flashlight, in a short night gown and no shoes on, watching us?"

She shook her head up and down!

Wow! No wonder she was feeling guilty!! She had been spying on us all along.

Michelle began to confess. She explained that she thought that if we knew she was up watching, we would go back to bed, and miss out on the fun evening.

Now that I think about it, I remember hearing strange noises, every now and then, during the three-hour "BUG hunt." "She," meaning the spy, wanted to hear Caroline's comments concerning the wedding albums earlier in the evening, so like spies do, she moved, crawling on the floor in the dark, to get closer to us so that she could hear what Caroline was saying.

Remember we were being sooo quiet because we didn't want to wake anyone up. Ha! The spy was already up! What a good example she turned out to be!?! Can't you just see her, on all fours, crawling on the floor with a short night gown on, no shoes and no flashlight! What a sight this would have been to see! I still can't believe this happened!

I wonder if "the spy" was ever planning to confess to us. I wonder if "the spy" felt guilty. I really think so. I would have loved for her to have joined the two of us. We really did have fun, and it would have been even more fun had she joined us.

Soon we were all talking at the same time and laughing at the end of the sentences. Everything was finally back to normal.

When we shared with Allison the story of our "BUG hunt," she said she wished she had been included. She thought eating the homemade ice-cream sundaes in the middle of the night was the best part of the entire evening. So I told both of them that the next time I visit their home in Texas, I will come prepared with chocolate syrup and ice cream and three trusty red-and-black Georgia flashlights, and I will wake them both up in the middle of the night to hunt for BUGS. "Bugs come out in the dark, you know," added Caroline.

You also must know that all things are bigger in Texas, so we will probably not have too much trouble seeing the BUGS. And, I think that, if Michelle continues to be a good mom, and takes care of the family, then we may, I mean may, let her go on the next "BUG hunt" with us. But it is possible that she might "be in the way." After all, she may not be able to keep up with the three of us.

One thing is for certain. On the next "BUG hunt," we will not need any shoes, but we will need our short night gowns, and I will most definitely bring the trusty red-and-black Georgia flashlights. However, there will be a slight twist. Instead of including Crystal the dog, we'll have Persy the cat.

I can truthfully say that I am personally looking forward to the next "BUG hunt" in the dark, way, way, way past midnight with my girls.

Well, it's been a long day and a very short night. However, this book is a book and as stated on page 1, Chapter 1 (Mimi to the Rescue)..."Once Upon a Time" always ends with "and they all lived happily ever after!"

The End

Do You Want to Play School?

Instructions:

1. Read the story aloud or silently.
2. One person will ask questions.
3. One person or more will answer the questions.
4. Look the answers up in the book.

Good luck! Have fun! Take turns being the teacher!
(Each question counts 4 points)

A = 90 - 100 points

B = 80 - 90 points

C = 70 - 80 points

D = 60 - 70 points

F = oops!

Questions:

1. How many times did you see a bug in the story?

2. What was the little sister's name?

3. Where did the story take place?

4. Who created the New York scrapbook?

5. What is the grandmother's nick name?

6. What did they dance on, that was wet?

7. Who ate ice cream?

8. Who ate lots of chocolate syrup and just a little ice cream?

9. Who wanted to go on the "Bug hunt" next time?

10. How many times in the entire short story was this group of words mentioned: "trusty, red-and-black Georgia flashlight?"

11. Who is Persy?

12. Does the grandmother have a red hat on?

13. Are bugs easy to see in the dark with a flashlight?

14. Who wrote Joanne Dillard Addison's Biography?

15. What time of night did the story begin?

16. What kind of dog is the grandma's dog?

17. Does the grandmother have shoes on?

18. What town does this story take place in?

19. What is the last sentence of the story?

20. How does the story begin?

21. How many grandchildren does Mimi have?

22. What is the Addison's dog's name?

23. Who made Mimi beautiful?

24. What does it mean: Write the alphabet in space?

25. What is an "ottoman"?

Answers are on the next page.

Answers:

1. Ten
2. Allison
3. Tuckertown
4. Julianna
5. Mimi
6. Deck floor
7. Caroline
8. Mimi
9. Allison
10. 16
11. The grandchildren's cat
12. No
13. Yes
14. Caroline
15. Midnight
16. Pekingese
17. No
18. Tuckertown
19. And everyone lived happily ever after.
20. Once upon a time
21. 10
22. Crystal
23. Remza
24. Write the letters in the air with your arms
25. A foot prop